MW00945603

FERAL

A Real Man, 7

Jenika Snow

FERAL (A Real Man, 7)
By Jenika Snow
www.JenikaSnow.com
Jenika_Snow@Yahoo.com
Copyright © December 2016 by Jenika Snow
First E-book Publication: December 2016

Photographer: Wander Aguiar :: Photography
Cover model: Jonny James
Photo provided by: Wander Book Club

Editors: Kasi Alexander / Lea Ann Schafer

ALL RIGHTS RESERVED: The unauthorized reproduction, trans-
mission, or distribution of any part of this copyrighted work is illegal.
Criminal copyright infringement is investigated by the FBI and is
punishable by up to 5 years in federal prison and a fine of $250,000.
This literary work is fiction. Any name, places, characters and inci-
dents are the product of the author's imagination. Any resemblance to
actual persons, living or dead, events or establishments is solely coin-
cidental.

Please respect the author and do not participate in or encourage pira-
cy of copyrighted materials that would violate the author's rights.

Book Layout © 2014 BookDesignTemplates.com

Feral/ Jenika Snow. -- 1st ed.

USA Today Bestselling Author

Jenika Snow

He'll show her exactly how much he wants her...

Feral

A Real Man

Everyone Needs A
REAL MAN

She's about to find out exactly how much he wants her…

Lexi

I've been fascinated with him for years.
He's wild and lives alone, and everyone has been smart
enough to keep their distance.

Except me, that is.

Until now.

I see something in him that I see in myself, and I want to
explore that. He's untamed and raw, and maybe dangerous.

But that's exactly what I need.

It's what I want.

Dillon

She shouldn't have come to me, but now that she's here, I
can't let her go.

I don't do well around others, so going off the grid has been
for the best.

What Lexi doesn't know is that I've noticed her for years and
wanted her as mine for just as long. It would be safer if I kept
her at a distance, which I've managed to do … but I can't
anymore.

I won't.

I hope she's ready to be mine, because she's about to see
exactly how feral I can be where it concerns her.

**Warning: This book is wild and dirty, short and smutty.
Sure, it's unbelievable, and features a celibate recluse who**

will make the woman he wants his at all costs, but who doesn't like it that way? If you are into an over the top alpha hero, and some filthy goodness, dive in.

CHAPTER ONE

Lexi

I knew he'd entered even though I wasn't looking up. The feel of the air changing around me and the sound of people whispering told me Dillon Sparrow had just walked into the grocery store where I worked. I lifted my head, not seeing him at first, but then noticing everyone was looking toward the back of the store.

And then I saw him.

He was big, seeming to take up the entire aisle he was in. The short-sleeved shirt he wore showed off the tattoos that covered his arms, and when he reached out to grab something off the shelf, I saw the ink on his hands. All those tattoos made him seem dangerous, although it wasn't the markings that had everyone talking and keeping away.

Dillon had a reputation in our town, one that had a lot of people staying back when he traveled down from his cabin in the middle of the woods. But what I didn't admit to anyone was that I looked forward to my monthly sightings of him. I anticipated them, hoping I was working when he came in.

And I was. Every single time.

"God, why does he come down here? He has to know everyone is afraid of him."

I glanced over at one of the other cashiers. She whispered to the stock boy, passing judgment on a man I knew she'd never even spoken with.

"Who is he?" the stock boy asked. He was new in town, but I was still surprised that he hadn't picked up on the gossip.

"Used to be a Marine. He was overseas, and when he came back, it was to find his younger brother dead."

My heart hurt in that moment. That was the actual truth.

"So why is everyone scared of him? I mean he's a beast, sure, but…"

"After he found his brother, he got drunk and beat the shit out of four guys. It was like nothing anyone had ever seen."

I ran my hands over my jeans, my palms sweaty.

"He did that for no reason?"

The cashier shrugged. "No one really knows. But he sent them all to the hospital." She lowered her voice. "If the cops hadn't shown up, he probably would have killed them. I'll tell you this, that man is dangerous and probably killed his brother himself."

"Shut the fuck up, Mary," I found myself saying, the words tumbling out of my mouth on their own.

Mary, an older lady, looked at me with wide eyes.

"All you do is talk shit." Heat filled me after I told her off. It felt good, empowering.

I looked over to where Dillon was. He had to be acutely aware that people talked about him, had to feel their gazes and hear their whispers. But he always kept to himself when he came down from the mountain. No one knew why he'd gone off the deep end. There were, of course, rumors about issues he'd had while deployed, or that he'd lost his shit when he found his brother—the only remaining family he had—dead.

But no one knew the real truth, and to be honest it wasn't anyone's business. I don't know why I found Dillon so fascinating. Maybe it was because he didn't have anyone either. With my mother passing just last year, and no siblings or really any extended family, I was truly alone in this world.

Just like him.

I couldn't help myself from staring at him a little longer. He kept his head down unless it was to grab something off the shelf.

I felt pissed because of the way he was treated, at the fact people kept a wide berth form him like he had the plague.

Then do something about it. Talk to him. Make him see he's not this outcast that should feel like shit when he comes to town to get supplies.

Of course I didn't think he gave two shits about what anyone said.

But when I glanced up at him, I was surprised to see Dillon staring right at me. His dark gaze locked on mine, and a chill raced up my spine. The feeling I got was pretty intense.

I turned and made myself busy because I didn't want to be one of those people who gawked, but also because I felt weird in my own skin right now. It wasn't an uncomfortable sensation, so to speak, but one that made me highly aware of what was going on around me.

I didn't know how long I "kept myself busy," but when I felt someone behind me, I turned, ready to help the customer. I didn't even have to look up to know Dillon was at my register. I saw his hands first. They were so big, tattooed, and powerful. They made me think of erotic things, of what I wanted him to do to me with them.

Touching me.

Holding me.

Keeping me down as he took what he wanted.

I shivered at the thoughts and images that slammed into my head.

I ran my gaze along his abdomen. I could see how strong he was under the shirt, the ridges and outline of his muscles beneath that thin gray material. He was tall, muscular, but not so huge that it was grotesque. His power was lean and intense.

And then I looked into his face. The black facial hair only added to how mysterious he appeared.

Then there were his eyes: dark, brooding, seeming to spear right into the very essence of my soul.

I was aware of others watching, maybe wondering what was wrong with me. I was frozen in place, unable to move or think rationally. But then again I felt like this every time he came in … every time he picked my register out of all the others.

I started ringing him up because I needed something to do or I'd just stare at him.

Does he feel that spark of electricity between us, too?

Focus on the checkout. Don't seem like another off-balanced citizen of this fucked-up town.

Batteries.

Canned food.

Nonperishable items.

Alcohol.

I focused on the groceries he'd gotten, but I felt him watching me. It was like he reached out and touched me.

Once I had everything scanned, I looked at him and stated his total. For a second he didn't say anything, just stared into my eyes. But then he reached into his wallet and handed me the cash. Our fingers brushed together when I took it from him.

The words I'd wanted to say each and every time he came to the store were right on the tip of my tongue. But instead of saying them, I got his change and handed it back.

Right before he left, I felt the courage rise up.

"Don't worry about what anyone else says. Not everyone likes judging others."

He stopped and turned to face me. Still he kept quiet.

I felt stupid for having mentioned anything, but a part of me was glad I had.

"What makes you think I worry about what these assholes say about me?" He showed no emotion on his face.

I swallowed, feeling my face heat at his words. "I don't think you do care." I ran my hands down my pants again, my nerves setting in. "I don't judge," I said. God, I was so nervous, and his eyes felt like daggers in my side. "I just wanted you to know." Fuck all my coworkers watching this interaction. I was done being quiet and pretending like this town wasn't one cesspool of hateful gossip.

"Thank you," he finally said, and I swear my entire body lit up like it had just been set on fire. He grabbed his bags and left without saying anything else.

I stood there for a second, barely able to breathe. Then I looked around and saw coworkers and customers alike staring at me.

Yeah, fuck them all.

Dillon

I watched her while I sat inside my truck. Her dark hair was piled high on her head, and the flush that stole over her face when she'd spoken to me was starting to fade.

She fascinated me, had for years, but I was smart enough and had enough self-control, that I didn't even fucking go there.

She's too young for me.

She's too innocent for what I want to do to her.

Little Lexi Brandon doesn't need a man like me in her life.

I ran a hand over my face. I came to town once a month strictly for supplies, or at least that's what everyone thought. Truth was I did come down for supplies, but I also came down to see *her*.

But my life hasn't been easy, and I wasn't stable on the best of days. I had a lot of demons I fought, and so moving out to the middle of fucking nowhere was my best option to live some kind of productive life.

But none of that, not even the thoughts of wanting to protect her—from myself—could stop me from craving Lexi.

Despite my best judgment and telling myself I needed to leave her alone and not obsess, I knew what I had to do.

I knew what I wanted to do. Although I could have just made my point now, made her mine now, I didn't want to scare the fuck out of her.

I wasn't a total heathen. Well, I didn't want to be one with her.

I wanted her to desire me as much as I did her. Even though I was in the mind to just throw her over my shoulder and haul her back to my cabin like some caveman carrying his prize, I also had an abundance of patience.

She'd be mine, one way or another.

CHAPTER TWO

Lexi

One week later

I wasn't a child that didn't know what I wanted in life. But I was ignorant about what I could have. Because what I desperately wanted was to know who the real Dillon Sparrow was.

And that's exactly what I planned on doing.

I grabbed my hiking pack off the floor by the door, turned, and looked at the quiet, lonely house I'd grown up in. I exhaled. I'd isolated myself so much since my mother's death. What little friends I did have were now gone, moving on with their lives. I had no one to tell me this was a bad idea.

And it probably was a very bad idea, but I was done sitting here feeling sorry for myself.

I didn't even know Dillon aside from the things I'd heard about him through the rumor mill.

I wasn't waiting another month for him to come into town to take action. My fascination with him might make me do foolish things, but I was ready to find my own answers.

I shut my front door, made my way to my car, and climbed in. My heart was thundering, and I honestly had no idea what I'd do when I got to the mountains.

I knew he lived off Crystal Lane, a small dirt road that ascended the mountain before stopping. The road just ended; then I'd have to hike. I prayed I was leaving early enough to make it there before nightfall.

Then what? Just show up at his door saying I'm crazy enough to break through the privacy he clearly wants?

I shook my head and sat with my hands on the steering wheel, rethinking this.

This is a bad idea.

I'd either find the things I was looking for and tame this curiosity I had for him, or...

This would be the worst mistake I ever made.

Dillon

Lexi's been mine since the first moment I saw her.

She was on my mind constantly, this need I couldn't shake.

I didn't want to try and stop myself from thinking about her though.

I wanted it to consume me until there wasn't anything left, until I was just a shell of a man grasping for the reality of my life.

She's that reality.

Seeing her every month was a light to my darkness, a spike of pleasure to the coldness of my heart.

I obsessed about her, wanted to possess every inch of her. I wanted Lexi to look into my face and know I owned her irrevocably. It was sheer self-control and the need to protect her—even from myself—that had me staying away.

I never claimed to be a good man.

I *didn't* want to be a good man.

Even if I wanted to, I couldn't give her that happily ever after.

The other part of me was just a territorial bastard when it came to her.

What I could provide was a twisted fairy tale that made her understand she was it … that she was the only one that would ever matter.

You're fucking crazy to think she'd want you, that she'd want anything to do with you.

There were rumors in town about me, some fabricated out of fear but mostly all true.

What did she think about that? Did she fear me too? Did she wonder how far I could go, how broken I really was?

I scrubbed a hand over my face, feeling the facial hair scrape across my palm. I'd waited a long time, held back from going after what I wanted … her. But the anticipation of having her as mine ate at me, made me tear at my insides, and had me desperate for her.

I'd waited long enough. It was time to make my move, to show Lexi what we could have together. I'd go to her, make her see I wanted her … always.

She'd find out exactly how far I was willing to go to make sure she stayed by my side. Because when it came to her, I was feral.

Lexi

Sweat covered my body, and I was having a hard time breathing the higher I ascended the mountain.

I'd been walking for the last … I didn't even know. My legs hurt, my feet ached, and I was seriously starting to reconsider this idea.

I had to be close. I'd followed the path, but the sun was hidden above the treetops, and I knew it would be setting soon.

How stupid and desperate do I have to be to think this is a good idea?

I adjusted my bag on my shoulder. At least I wasn't dumb enough not to bring a couple of water bottles with me. I sat on a boulder, resting my feet and staring at the path. Maybe I should just head back, call this a bust, and decide what exactly I needed in my life.

After taking a long drink of water, I stared up at the trees. A slight breeze blew by, making the branches sway back and forth. It was peaceful up here, with just nature and my thoughts to keep my company. But for as beautiful as this all was, it was getting dark, I didn't know how far off I was, and I wanted to just go home.

How could I have thought showing up at some random man's house was the best-laid plan? How did I think Dillon would even welcome something like this?

The sound of a twig snapping close by had me standing. My heart raced, and my entire body became alert. I scanned my surroundings, but of course I saw nothing. Every horror movie I'd ever seen slammed through my head.

A serial killer.

A deranged psycho.

A wild animal intent on using me as a chew toy.

A werewolf.

All those thoughts and images had my heart beating harder, faster. To run or not to run...

Hell, it could have just been an animal. I was in the middle of the woods.

Where no one can hear me, and if I go missing, I might never be found.

I didn't think anymore, just walked quickly back down the mountain. Fuck all of this. I might want desperately to know Dillon, but I also didn't want to die in the process.

The sound of something running over the underbrush had me picking up my pace. I glanced behind me and saw nothing.

My fear rose higher.

I did run then, even though I thought that might only make this worse. I glanced over my shoulder, and that's when I saw it.

A fucking squirrel.

I felt really damn stupid then and chuckled at myself. But just as I was about to slow and catch my breath, I tripped. I fell forward fast and hard, and the pain lasted a second before blackness took me under.

CHAPTER THREE

Dillon

I tracked.
I hunted.
I killed for my meals.

It was the life I chose to live, the way I decided to survive. The supplies I got from town were nonperishables and essential hygiene products. But meat, protein … that I found on my own. That I worked to get.

I also came down to get my disability check. It didn't allow me to live in luxury, but then again I didn't want to. I was a simple man with simpler needs.

I moved through the forest silently, making sure to scan my surroundings. I'd been tracking a deer for the last hour. It was close. I could feel the fear in the air, the fact that it knew it was being tracked.

I'd been doing this long enough this was second nature to me, something that was a part of me. For more than a decade I'd been out here, by myself. Being around people wouldn't do me any good. With my brother gone and no other family, I was alone. But I had become used to it.

But wanting Lexi and knowing I could have her were two very different things.

And I would have her.

I stopped, listening. I heard the deer to my left and started going that way. My bow was at my side, my body ready, my heart rate slow, steady.

I was close to the path that led all the way up to my cabin, and moved toward it. And then I saw the animal. I crouched low, partially hidden behind a large tree. I got my bow ready.

Its head was raised, and its ears twitched. It knew I was here, but didn't know where or how dangerous I was. This wasn't a game to me. This was survival, food.

I was about to take aim when the sound of a female moan had me freezing. The deer ran off and I cursed, but the sound came again and I rose up and made my way toward it. I was close enough to see the path, but I didn't see anyone on it.

And then I saw her.

Lexi.

Out here in the middle of nowhere.

Hurt.

I attached my bow to my back and made my way quickly toward her. My heart was at a steady pace, but every instinct in me was roaring to get to her. I needed to protect her.

I crouched in front of her and instantly saw the blood on her temple. She was on her belly, the rock she must have hit just an inch from her skull. She moaned again, but her eyes were closed.

I didn't think about anything else but getting Lexi to my cabin and making sure she was okay. Town was too far away, and I wanted her surrounded by my things while I tended to her.

Territorial.

Possessive.

Mine.

Lexi

I felt something wet on my face right before full consciousness woke me. Or maybe it was the wetness that roused me?

"Lexi?"

The voice I heard was deep, husky. It was familiar.

"Lexi, open your eyes for me, baby."

I did as I was gently commanded. My vision was blurry at first, but then it cleared and I saw Dillon in front of me. He helped me sit up, and I grimaced as my head pounded. I lifted my hand and touched the bandage that was on my temple.

"What happened?" I asked. My voice was hoarse, and I cleared it. He handed me a glass of water, and I drank it down. I hadn't realized I'd been so thirsty until I'd seen it.

"Here," he said and handed me two white pills.

I eyed them and then lifted my head and looked at Dillon.

"It's acetaminophen. I'm sure your head is killing you."

He didn't show any emotion, didn't have any expression. His face was like granite.

"Thank you." I took the pills and washed them down with the remaining water. He had the glass refilled seconds later. I finished off that one, too.

"You must have fallen and hit your head on a rock. I found you while hunting." My head throbbed as if his words were the reminder it needed. "But it appears superficial. I don't think you have a concussion, but if you want, I can take you to the hospital in town."

I stared into his eyes. I didn't want to go anywhere, even if I was hurt. I touched my head again. That one spot was tender, but otherwise I felt okay. "Was I out long?"

"I found you a few hours ago."

I glanced at the only window I saw. It was pitch-black outside. After handing the glass back to him, I watched as he made his way into what I assumed was the kitchen. There was a wood-burning stove, an ancient-looking icebox, and a makeshift sink. As I looked around, I realized this entire place was pretty rustic. He had one couch that had seen better days, and nothing electric that I could spot. I continued to take in my surroundings.

The cabin was small, tiny really. It was one large room, and the bed I was in took almost the entire left corner. But Dillon was a large man, and I didn't think a twin mattress would sustain him through the night. I stared at the fire, which he was in the process of stoking. My stomach let out this low rumble, and heat instantly filled my face.

Dillon turned around, but his face held no expression. "When was the last time you ate?"

I thought about it. I'd eaten a decent breakfast but had only snacked during the hike. "It's been a while," I said.

He made a gruff sound and nodded before turning and walking over to where the sink was. I just now realized he had a freezer off to the side. It had been partially hidden by the wall that came out slightly from the kitchen area.

Okay, so he clearly has electricity to run that thing.

"A generator."

I snapped my gaze from the freezer to him. He stared at me, his voice so deep it felt like it could actually stroke my flesh.

He pulled out a slab of what appeared to be meat, and my stomach decided to growl in that instant. Dillon glanced at me again, and although I saw something flash in his eyes, his expression remained stoic.

"Give me ten and I'll have something for you."

My head started pounding for a second before finally the pain relented. My feet were bare of shoes, but I was still in my hiking clothes. Then again, no matter what stories I'd heard about Dillon being a predator, he'd tended to me. He'd cared for me, and still was.

True to his words, ten minutes later he was walking back over with a plate in one hand and a freshly filled glass of water in the other.

"You think you're good to sit at the table?" He tipped his chin toward the small wooden table off to the side. There was only one chair pushed up against it, and it looked aged and worse for wear.

I nodded and pushed myself up. Even with socks on, the wooden floor was chilly under my feet. Dillon set the plate and glass down and pulled the chair out for me. When I was seated and he leaned down slightly and pushed it in, I swore I heard him inhale. But he straightened and walked around the table a second later.

He leaned against the back of the scarred, torn couch, his big arms crossed, his gaze on me. Even though I'd seen him plenty of times over the years, right now, right here seemed different. The gray long-sleeved shirt he wore was pushed up his tattooed forearms. I stared at his hands, inked as well, and imagined them once again on me, touching me, making me submit to his will. I lifted my gaze over his chest. The power seethed beneath the surface. I followed that strength up his inked throat and to his face. I swore I saw emotion flicker and make up his expression for a second.

"Thank you for helping me and making sure I was okay."

"You're welcome, Lexi."

The way he said my name had my skin coming alive.

"No matter what you've heard, I'm not a monster."

Although he said that, I watched this hard darkness cover his face.

"I never thought you were a monster." I'd come here for that reason, to tell him I wanted him, that we'd be good for each other in all ways. But right now it seemed so misplaced.

Right now didn't seem like the best time for it.

I focused on the food in front of me. He'd made me a steak. I started eating, my stomach growling again. Before I knew it, I'd eaten half of it. He came closer and pushed the glass of water toward me. I finished that as well.

"Thank you again."

He grunted in response and took the plate and glass away. "Lay back down. You hit your head pretty good.

Relaxing in bed for the rest of the night is probably best."

"My back and ass hurts from laying down." I went to stand, but a wave of dizziness assaulted me. I tipped slightly, the chair in my way causing me to go off balance. I thought I was about to hit the ground, but strong arms wrapped around my middle and pulled me back to a hard chest. For a second everything stilled.

I stopped breathing.

I heard my heart racing in my ears.

I felt the strength and maleness coming from him. The scent of him, and being surrounded by his things, slammed into me.

"Come on," he said softly, but with a voice so deep there was no doubt he was all man.

I might have been dizzy at this moment, but I sure as hell could feel every ridge and dip of his hard body.

He helped me to the bed, and once I was in it, the dizziness passed and I breathed out. I closed my eyes, exhaustion settling in. This should have felt weird, me lying in Dillon's bed, him tending to me.

But it didn't.

It actually felt … right and comfortable.

I knew Dillon was staring at me because I could feel his gaze on me. And when I opened my eyes, I saw I was correct. He stood by my side, his body so big, so powerful.

"What were you doing all the way out here?" he asked, and I struggled for a second on what to say. Be honest, or make up some bullshit excuse because telling him why I'd been so close to where he obviously lived seemed weird as hell?

In the end I decided to be honest. That was always the best course of action.

"I was looking for you." I shifted on the bed. Now resting on the pillows, my upper body propped up and my heart thundering because I'd admitted the truth, I waited for Dillon to say something.

He turned and grabbed the chair I'd just been sitting in and brought it close. The leg of it scraped along the wooden floor. The lighting in the cabin was all from lanterns and candles, and I found it a little odd, seeing as he did have a generator.

What's so strange about it? This man clearly likes to live off the grid, and he enjoys a simple existence. Ho many people can you say that about?

"Why?" he finally said, and I glanced down at my hands. I had them twisted together, my nerves coming to the surface.

"I've watched you come into the grocery store every month for years." I made eye contact with him. But Dillon was always a hard book to read. He didn't show any external emotions, so trying to gauge his reaction to this was impossible. "And every time I looked at you, heard the rumors, saw the way you didn't let it affect you, I knew you and I were the same."

He lifted a brow as if what I'd said was ridiculous. Although that expression was pretty guarded as well.

"So you thought it was smart coming all the way out here to what, tell me that?" He rested back on the chair and crossed his big arms over his chest. I shouldn't have taken that second to look at how wide his shoulders were or how broad his chest was. I also shouldn't have let my gaze linger on the clear definition of his six-pack under the thin material he had on.

But being in his presence made me feel like I was the most feminine person in the world, like compared to him, I was fragile.

"I didn't say it was the best plan," I admitted.

For long seconds neither of us said anything. But it wasn't this weird silence that descended. He watched me, and as much as I wanted to look away because the focus of someone staring at me was pretty intense, I stared right back. He shifted on his seat and leaned forward to rest his forearms on his thighs.

"What if I hadn't been hunting? What if I hadn't been there, Lexi?"

No words came to me at that moment.

"You know there are wild animals out here, ones that wouldn't have thought twice about going after you, especially with fresh blood in the air."

My throat went tight.

"The thought of something worse happening to you..." He stopped speaking then, his face going hard, as if he were pissed. "It would have been fucking devastating, Lexi."

God, the emotion in his voice was the most I'd ever seen or heard in all the years I'd known him.

He rested back on the chair again, his jaw tight, a muscle contracting and releasing under his stubble-covered flesh.

"We could have talked in town," he finally said again after long seconds of silence.

"We could have." I looked down at my hands again. I felt like a fool right now, like I was being scolded.

He's right though. What if something worse had happened? It was pure luck he came when he did.

God, I didn't even want to think about that. I just wanted to close my eyes and pretend that things were exactly how I'd envisioned them ... Dillon telling me he wanted this just as badly as I did.

CHAPTER FOUR

Dillon

Lexi had fallen asleep an hour ago, and although I wanted to tell her that being here, under my roof, in my space, was exactly where I wanted her, I'd kept my mouth shut.

She'd come out here to talk to me.

That realization had lust, intensity, and a slew of other emotions I'd always forced myself not to feel coming right to the surface.

She made this soft sound in her sleep, and I pushed my thoughts aside and looked at her. I didn't want her to go, and the thought of chaining her to my bed and keeping her here played through my mind. I wasn't a fucking creep, and even if I wanted her as mine no matter what, I wanted her here because she desired it.

She came to me. She wanted to talk with me.

True on every account, but how would she feel if I told her I'd been about to go down there and make it known I didn't want to have those passing glances once a month anymore? How would she feel if I admitted I'd been fighting my attraction to her, that what I really wanted to do was pin her to my bed, force her thighs as wide as they'd go, and plunge my cock into her? I'd claim every part of her, fill her with my cum so she smelled like me ... was marked by me.

I wanted that and so much more.

The years isolated from people had hardened me. I knew that.

I welcomed it, embraced it.

I never claimed to be the type of man that could give her a happily ever after, not one found in a fairy tale at least. But what I could give her, what I wanted to give her, was a life where she wasn't alone. I wanted to show her how devoted I could be, how I'd make sure she always came first.

My life had been lived in solitude for so long that I was ready to end that. I was ready to let myself feel something other than the crushing loneliness and anger I'd held on to for years.

I stared at Lexi but thought about my brother.

Dean had his problems. He always had. Before I'd been deployed, I'd tried to be there for him, to keep him busy, let him know he didn't have to resort to drugs to feel alive. He'd done well, went to rehab, and had a job, a place. He'd been clean and sober for three years. I was so fucking proud of him, and it was then I decided to start living my life.

I'd been selfish, and it was my fault he'd fallen back into the life he had.

I scrubbed a hand over my face and breathed out. I had so much fucking baggage I was drowning in it. It would never go away, never disappear. I'd always have it latched on to me like a parasite, and no matter how much I buried it or covered it with my own darkness, it would always be a part of me.

But then there was Lexi. We hadn't even spent one full day in each other's company, yet I felt this lightness when I was around her. I felt this need to keep her with me, no matter what, but I also knew if I was going to make this work, to make her see she belonged with me, I'd have to be honest about the type of man I was, and that I'd go to any lengths to get what I wanted.

And I'd never wanted anything more than her.

Lexi
The following day

I'd woken up not realizing where I was at first. But it had only taken a moment for me to remember the hit to the head, Dillon, and everything that had come after that. But then again, there hadn't been much that happened after he'd cooked me dinner. I'd been so tired, and although I'd wanted to talk with him, open up about everything, I'd fallen asleep.

Thank goodness I found the bathroom in the cabin. It was just a toilet in the corner, a tiny sink next to that, and a makeshift curtain to give privacy.

I stood, the wooden floor so damn cold. A fire was already started, and I walked over to it. With my hands out in front of me, the warmth seeping into my flesh, I thought about what I was going to do.

The morning light shone through the window. I was alone in the cabin, but I had a feeling Dillon wasn't that far off. And then I saw him. He stood by a shed, the double doors open, and a deer carcass hanging on the inside. I covered my mouth, my stomach roiling.

Of course I wasn't a stranger to hunting and what went with it, but still, witnessing it all, the cuts, the skin peeling back, all of it was unsettling.

I turned from it and scanned the cabin. It seemed bigger in the daylight, and for the first time I noticed a small loft above. Curious, I went over to the ladder that was pushed off to the side and climbed it. My head didn't hurt too bad this morning, and I knew I'd have to face the fact that he'd probably kick me out.

This isn't your home, though, no matter how much you want to be with Dillon.

When I reached the top, I was surprised to see it was a reading nook. Several small bookshelves were positioned around a long chair that sat in the center of the floor. The legs look liked they'd been cut from the chair, making it flush with the ground. Then again, the roof was an A-shape design, and for a man like Dillon, who was exceptionally tall, he'd still have to crouch while up here.

I didn't want to be nosy, but the fact that this man spent his time reading up here alone did something to my heart.

I heard a ruckus outside and climbed back down. When I was in front of the window again, I saw Dillon shutting the doors to the shed. Blood covered his light-colored shirt, but before I could think about anything else, he was removing it.

God.

He rolled the shirt up into a ball, and with the clean side he ran the material over his face. It was cold outside, and I could see his breath fanning out in front of him, but I also saw sweat lining his forehead and chest. My heart thundered, and I felt it in my throat. He was all raw muscle, powerful, dangerous. I felt every feminine cell in my body come alive. He called to my basic urges, my need to just let go of every preconceived notion of what was going to happen and how I wanted it to go.

I should have turned and not gawked, but I was a slave to the sight of him He walked around the side of the shed and disappeared. I turned and rested my back against the wall right by the window. A choice needed to be made. I'd either push away any notion of what I wanted with him, or come clean before it was too late. Figuring that out sooner rather than later was for the best.

CHAPTER FIVE

Dillon

I'd seen her watching me as I took care of the deer, and felt her gaze on me when I'd taken off the filthy shirt and wiped myself down. I fucking loved that she stared at me, and hoped like hell it got a reaction out of her.

There was a lot I'd do today concerning her. Lexi would know I wanted her as mine before the day was over with. And if she thought she'd just walk out of here … she'd find out soon enough I wouldn't let her go without a fight.

I stepped out of the small building I'd erected for the shower. The cabin itself was void of electricity, and although through the years I could have easily rigged it so I could use the generator for more than the freezer, I preferred this simple way of living.

The shower was fed from a cistern and heated by a manual fire I didn't light more times than not.

I dried off, grabbed the change of clothes I kept in the shower shed, and headed back to the cabin. My body was revved up, thoughts on what I wanted to do with Lexi and what I wanted to say to her running through me a mile a minute.

Hell, I should have just kept my bloody clothes on so she could see the outside version of that darkness I held in me. It would have been more honest than cleaning up, like I was attempting to wash away the grisly reality of the person I was.

She'd either be down for what I wanted, or I'd scare the fuck out of her.

Either way I'd find out.

I stepped into the cabin and saw her looking through the cupboards in the kitchen. I shut the door, the sound of being enclosed making an audible *click*, like a snicker of the situation that was about to go down.

She turned and stared at me, her eyes wide, her nerves right on the surface. I glanced at the table: a large bowl, spoon, flour, sugar, and a few other items littered the top.

"What are you doing?" I asked curiously.

She started rubbing her hands down her pants. "I figured I'd keep myself busy and make you something to eat. It's the least I can do to say thanks for helping me." She looked at the items on the table. "I mean, using your shit and all." She chuckled nervously, and when she realized I hadn't moved or said anything, I saw her nerves jack up a degree.

"I'm not hungry." Not for food at least.

I'm hungry for you, though.

"Oh," she said and looked uncomfortable.

Despite the fact that I'd never cared about what anyone said, nor how they felt—especially if I was the one who made them feel awkward—I wanted Lexi to know she was different. "Thank you though. That was a nice gesture." My voice was hard, gruff. In this moment it took a lot of fucking control not to just claim her right here and now. But, I wasn't some sick fuck. She'd hurt her head and needed to rest.

Showing emotion was never something I was good at. "Did you eat the granola and fruit I set out for you?" I stepped farther into the cabin. I wanted her to get her strength up.

She'll need all the strength she can get for what I have planned.

It was just that one thought that broke through my carefully placed control. My cock jerked behind my jeans, and I willed the fucker to stay down.

I watched her as she went over to the table and started picking things up, presumably to put them away.

"Leave them," I said, harder than I'd intended. She instantly froze, then took a step back. My cock jerked again at the fact that she obeyed so well.

I moved closer, stalking her, my focus solely on the way she reacted to me right now. I saw the beat of her pulse under her ear. It was rapid, frantic. I saw the way she breathed harder, faster. I looked down to see her twisting her fingers together, her nervousness tangible.

"You killed a deer this morning?" she asked, her voice shaking slightly.

I was pretty sure there was nothing but arousal coming from her. It was the way she looked at me, and she wasn't very good at hiding her emotions.

Her facial expression spoke volumes, and I fucking loved it.

"Yes. I left you sleeping early this morning. I needed the meat to store for winter." It was cold as fuck out, and it would only get worse with each passing day. This type of living didn't have me stocking my freezer with pre-packaged meat.

I went out and killed for it.

I moved a step closer. I'd left her sleeping in my bed while I went out, but truth was I'd wanted nothing more than to slip in beside her, remove her clothing, and spread her legs before plunging my cock into her tight heat.

Giving up my bed and sleeping on the couch was a hardship only because I wanted beside her so damn badly.

I want in *her.*

Fuck, I was harder than granite, and when I saw Lexi look down at my crotch, I knew there was no trying to hide that I wanted her.

I don't want to hide it, because right now she's going to know exactly what I desire.

"There are some things that need to be said," I told her, moving another step closer.

She nodded and licked her lips, and I stared at the pink plumpness of her mouth. Filthy images slammed into my mind: her lips wrapped around my dick, her jaw wide to take the length and girth.

Shit, I could practically feel the tip of my shaft hitting the back of her throat as I face fucked her. I'd own every part of her. I'd claim her cunt, make her ass mine. I'd come on her belly and watch as she rubbed it in, marking herself with my spunk, smelling like me.

"And when I tell you these things, you're going to have to make up your mind on what you want to do." I clenched my hands at my sides, the desire to just go up to her, strip her of her clothes, and lift her up and over my shoulder, riding me hard.

I visualized my hand going down on her ass, making the mound shake and turn red. My handprint would stay on her flesh as I fucked her, but she'd like that. She'd want more of it.

"Okay," she finally said, whispering the word.

Yeah, once I finally told her everything, admitted who I was and what I wanted, we'd see exactly how far she was willing to go.

CHAPTER SIX

Lexi

I stared at Dillon. He looked especially fierce right now, like a wild animal was trapped within him, desperate to get out.

It seemed like long moments before he finally spoke again.

"I don't want you to leave."

My heart thundered harder at his words. He didn't want me to go. Good, because I didn't want to.

"But I need you to know about me, about my past and the type of man I am."

The way he said that made it sound so ominous.

I nodded slowly. I assumed he was referring to the rumors I'd heard, or maybe what had gone down with his brother. "We all have demons in our closet."

He was silent for so long I felt this weird sensation move through me.

"I've killed people, Lexi."

I assumed as much. He was a Marine, after all. "Being in the military and fighting for your life surely didn't give you a lot of options."

"And you think that makes it okay?" He lifted a dark brow, his face still void of emotion.

"No, but it's a fact of life, and it doesn't make you a monster." I didn't even know if this was where the conversation was going. "I'm sure you didn't have a choice," I said again.

He stopped advancing and stared at me. For long seconds he didn't speak, and I wondered if he was trying to come up with reasoning on why what he had to do made him the devil.

"Everyone has a choice," was all he said in reply. "I left my brother alone. He had a history of substance abuse, depression. I shouldn't have left. It's because of me he overdosed. It's because of me he's gone." His voice was thick, and I heard emotion in it. He tried to mask it, to appear strong—and he was—but right now I could see him … the real him.

"If you're trying to vilify yourself to me, it's not going to work." I stared him right in the eyes. "I've seen you come into that grocery store every month, keep your head down, and ignore the whispering and comments about you." I moved closer to him.

"Why did you really come out here? Why did you leave the safety of others, of your home, and come after a man that for all you know wanted to hurt you?"

I felt my eyebrows going down, my confusion and worry filling every part of me that he'd actually think that.

"I've seen the look of sorrow in your eyes, pain, that expression of emptiness that you try so hard to hide." I shook my head. "You can't hide it from someone who feels it too." I was only a few feet from him now, and the scent of his cologne—or maybe it was just his natural, woodsy aroma—slammed into me. "I came out here because I wanted to be around someone who gets it, who's like me." I hesitated for just a second, but then said fuck my caution. I lifted my hand and placed it right over his heart. "You lost the only family you had left. I know how that feels."

He placed his hand over mine.

"People can make their own choices. I did by coming out here. And your brother did as well." I didn't want to open a wound that was obviously not healed, but I wanted him to see I didn't look at him like some kind of monster. "You didn't kill your brother. You wanted to live your life. We all do." He flexed his hand over mine, and I felt my heart jump. I really hoped I wasn't crossing any lines or thinking I knew anything more than I did. I just wanted Dillon to see that the world keeps going, even if we are stuck at the bottom.

He leaned in close, his face only an inch from mine now. "I *am* a monster, but you only want to see the good in me." He let go of my hand, and I retreated. The darkness he held like a second skin was back in place. "I'll always be this way, Lexi. I'll always need to be alone, to keep away from people unless absolutely necessary." He took a step closer to me, and I moved one back. "I'll never change." The way he looked at me was heated, dangerous. "And as much as I want to just let everything go, to let your sweet, positive words sink in, I can't."

I was breathing harder.

"But I will say this." He moved even closer, and I found myself stepping back, unable to stop myself. "I know what I want, and that's you."

Dillon

I stepped closer to her, watching as she retreated. She was afraid of me, afraid of everything I'd told her. She saw the darkness in me. I felt it, sensed it from her like she was this wounded, frightened creature lost in the woods.

It made me harder.

"You fear me," I stated bluntly.

"No," she whispered.

But I could see it in her eyes. It wasn't the kind of fear that had her thinking I'd hurt her. No, it was the kind that she produced because she was afraid of how she felt in this moment ... what she wanted with me.

I was a hunter, a feral man living out in the fucking middle of nowhere because I preferred being on my own to being around others. I tracked, hunted, and killed for my meals. I could see the signs on her body as easily as I could feel my heart beating in my chest right now.

She stopped with her hands pressed to the wall behind her, and I watched as she held her breath. It was subtle, just an inhalation ... then no exhalation. She held it for a few seconds as she stared at me; then she slowly breathed out. I lowered my gaze to her throat, saw her pulse beating hard, fast.

She was nervous but aroused.

I bet her pussy was wet for me. I bet if I touched her, she'd give in to me just like that.

I kept my focus on her. I didn't want to miss the slightest emotion flickering across her face. Her lips were slightly parted, and I could hear her increased breathing. I was a foot from her, the sweet scent of her like nothing I'd ever smelled. My cock was so fucking hard, like a damned steel pipe behind my jeans.

"I don't want you to be afraid of me, even though you should."

"I'm not afraid of you."

I heard the truth in her voice, but still, she was so much better than me. She was sweet and kind and hadn't seen the disgust of the world like I had.

She's lost like me, and has known pain and loneliness, too.

"What do you want?" I asked slowly, my voice low. "Tell me what you want." I needed to hear her admit she wanted this, that she wanted me. Because right now I was lost in my desire for her. I was gone from the need to have her in every way, to make her feel good.

I was aching to hear those words spill from her lips, like a vocal surrender before I claimed her body.

But she didn't answer me right away. It was equal disappointment and arousal. The fact that she was resisting, trying to be strong, turned me on. But I was also a man who wanted what only she could give.

I stepped closer, my chest right up against hers, so that if I inhaled deeply it would brush along hers. I lowered my gaze, watched as her chest rose and fell fast, her breathing increased, her emotions raw. I was good at picking out the little things, the subtle changes in someone. Maybe it was my training in the military, or maybe it was just this woman who made everything in me more heightened?

Either way I'd get what I wanted from her, not because I'd force it out of her, but because I'd make her realize that what she needed from me, I was freely giving.

She had yet to answer me.

"Resisting what I want only turns me on, Lexi." I lifted my gaze and stared at her face. Fuck, her pupils were so dilated. I knew she was ready for me, her body primed to take what only I could give. The sound she made was a little bit of shock and pleasure. I heard it as well as if I had made it myself.

I lowered my hand, slid my fingers along the shirt she wore and stopped when I got to the hem. For a second I just left the digits there and stared into her eyes. The anticipation and excitement of what I was about to do raced through my veins. I was amped up, needing this so damn badly I could taste it.

I curled my fingers under the hem of the shirt and slowly started to lift it up.

"So, tell me what you want and it's yours," I said on a groan.

"I want you. God," she finally said, the word nothing more than a breath of air from her parted lips.

I leaned in close so my mouth was right by hers. "No, not God, baby. Say *my* name." I went for the button of her pants, and because I was feral right now I had them undone and pushed down her thighs a second later. She made this noise that turned me on even more. "Take them off," I ordered, and I was pleased she obeyed instantly.

I had her shirt pushed up once more, and slipped my fingers lower until I felt the edge of her panties. I started to descend again, my fingers skimming her bare skin. I felt her flesh start to pucker from my touch, and the realization that she was so receptive to me pleased me to no end. "Say my name, Lexi," I commanded, staring right into her eyes.

"Dillon," she whispered.

I couldn't stop myself from groaning. Fuck, hearing her say my name did all kinds of things to me, had all sorts of filthy images slamming into my head.

"I've…"

I stared into her eyes, wanting her to tell me everything. I wanted her to divulge her deepest needs and wants.

I want to be the one who makes them her reality.

"Tell me," I demanded.

"I want this."

Yeah, she fucking did.

"But I've never done this before."

I clenched my jaw, a deep sound of pleasure leaving me.

"I've never been with a man."

She was a virgin, and I'd be the one to claim her cherry. I'd be the *only* one to know how her pussy felt, how tight and hot she really was. She might not know it yet, but Lexi was mine. She'd always be mine.

I couldn't stop myself from what I did next. I didn't even want to try.

"I'm going to show you what a real man does when he sees something he wants." I leaned down and closed my eyes, smelling her. I ran the tip of my nose up the arch of her neck. She shivered for me and made the sweetest fucking noise. The sound speared right to my dick and had my balls drawing up. I wanted to push into her, feel her virgin pussy clenching at my cock, milking me. I wanted to fill her up with my cum, make her so full of my seed that it slipped from the tight, hot confines of her body.

When I slid my hand along her outer thigh, she reached up and grabbed on to my biceps. I could tell it was an involuntary reaction given the expression on her face, but I fucking loved it just the same.

While holding her gaze, I slipped my hand along the back of her knee, lifted her leg easily, and wrapped it around my waist. She held it there like a good girl, and I moved my hand to cup her ass. The cheek was round ... perfect. I wanted her to feel how hard I was, how much I wanted her. My cock throbbed, and this wild need inside of me was like a living entity. It was more pressure than I'd ever felt before.

Not having sex had never been an issue for me, because the one I'd wanted had always been unattainable.

Not anymore. She's right here for the taking. She wants you to make her yours.

I wanted my mouth on hers, on her flesh, on her pussy. I wanted to memorize every single inch of her with my lips and tongue. There wouldn't be any part of her that I didn't own when I was finished with her.

Without tormenting myself any more, I moved down and onto my haunches in front of her. She had her arms by her sides now, her legs slightly parted. She looked down at me, her breathing still increased, her need still evident.

I could smell her, a sweet, musky scent that told me she was definitely soaked between her thighs. How pink would her pussy be? How wet would she continue to get for me? I looked up at her, and while staring into her eyes, I slipped my hand between her legs and placed it right over her pussy.

She gasped and slammed her hands behind her on the wall as if she needed that extra stability.

"I'm going to own this tonight." I added a little pressure, and she rose onto her toes. "And when I take your cherry, Lexi, you'll be mine irrevocably." I moved her panties to the side, feeling how wet the fabric was for me. "When I plunge my cock in your virgin cunt, no other man will have you. Ever." I ran a finger down her center, trying in vain to stay in control. My whole body was tight, the wild need to pull my cock out and take her right up against the wall riding me hard.

Her first time might not be as soft and gentle, or as romantic as she deserved. But I'd sure as fuck make sure she knew what she meant to me.

CHAPTER SEVEN

Dillon

"Please, I need you," she moaned, and I almost lost it right then. I nearly came without even being inside of her.

I hadn't been with a woman since I came back from active duty. I hadn't wanted to be with anyone, let alone have a female in my bed after the shit had gone down with my brother. But then I saw Lexi all those years ago, and my attraction had been instant.

And even if I did stay away, even if I had told myself not going after what I wanted—Lexi— was what was best for her, I couldn't stop myself anymore. I wanted her. Only her.

But then she'd spoken to me, the first time she'd ever done that. I'd looked into her eyes, seen something that was familiar, and I knew I was a stupid fuck for waiting, for not going after her.

"I had a lot of self-control back in the day when it came to you," I said right by her mouth.

"And now?"

"No. Fucking. Control."

She's mine.

I felt like a fucking animal with her right now, and all I wanted to do was devour every part of her. I wanted her to scream my name as I made her feel good. I wanted her to come for me as I licked every part of her body.

My cock jerked at the thought of all the things I'd do to her before the night was over with. And when morning did come, she'd still be here because I wasn't letting her go.

I saw her throat work as she swallowed. She was worked up, so fucking primed I knew if I touched her in just the right way, she'd come for me.

I knew she would ... craved to see that ecstasy morph her face.

There was no way I was going to last tonight, not once I was deep in her hot, wet, virgin pussy.

When it came to this woman right here, I was a fucking animal.

"I want you, Dillon."

I groaned, clenched my jaw, and prayed for some fucking restraint.

"I'm starving for you, Lexi, so fucking hungry I don't know if I can go slow." I moved closer. "And you want me, don't you?" I knew she did, but I wanted to hear her say it again. I wanted to hear her scream it out as she came for me.

She swallowed, and I watched the line of her throat work through the act.

"Tell me." I wanted to hear her say she wanted my big, thick cock in her. I wanted to see her lips form the words as she told me she wanted me to pop her cherry, to claim it as mine.

"I want to be yours in every way."

Holy. Fucking. Christ.

It took all my control not to get off right then and there, just come in my jeans from her words alone.

She licked her lips, and I was riveted to the sight. Filthy thoughts of her on her knees in front of me, using that little pink tongue to lick at my dick, to lap at the pre-cum that was already forming at the tip, slammed through my mind violently.

"You're so damn pretty, Lexi," I said, not able to help myself. I leaned forward and ran my tongue along the seam of her lips.

I was already addicted to her.

I had my hands by her head now, the wall cold, rough against my palms. I smelled the scent of her coating my fingers. It drove me crazy with need.

Because I was a vulgar bastard, I ground my hard dick right up against her belly. She made this little gasp, and I growled in approval. "You feel that?"

She had her head resting back on the wall, her mouth parted, and her eyes half-closed as her pleasure clearly washed through her.

"You see what you do to me? You see how hard you make me?"

"God. I need you."

"And you'll have me, every single part." I slipped my hand to her nape, curled my fingers into her soft flesh, and tilted her head to the side. I wanted to show her with my words, touch, with every part of me that we were made for each other.

I leaned down and ran my tongue along the side of her throat, feeling her pulse jack up higher, tasting the sweetness of her flesh.

"You feel good, baby?"

She nodded.

"God, but I'm going to make you feel even better." I licked at her throat again. "Hold on to me." She lifted her hands and placed them on my biceps, digging her nails into my flesh. My cock jerked at the pleasure and pain combination.

"I want you as mine forever," I admitted, not the least bit ashamed. I went back to dragging my tongue up the slender column of her throat. I could have done this all day and night, just got drunk from the flavor of her flesh, and the pleasure she gave me by making sweet, aroused little noises.

I thrust my cock against her belly, needing that friction like I needed to breathe.

I need her naked. I need her bared for me.

And then I started doing just that. I was a madman in this moment, so lost in wanting her that everything was a haze as I all but tore off her clothing. But she was so pliant, so receptive to what I did.

And when she was stark naked for me, I took a step back. I looked my fill, starting at her toes. I followed the lines of her long, slender legs, gazed at her pussy covered in a small, trimmed thatch of dark hair, moved my gaze along her belly button and flat stomach, and finally landed on her breasts.

Her tits were big, her nipples pink, elongated for me.

She was ready, and I knew she was wet, probably wetter than before.

I lifted my gaze to her face, saw how her pupils were dilated, and knew she wouldn't stop me.

"You want this in you?" I said crudely and grabbed my dick through my jeans. I was painfully hard, my dick like steel between my legs. My balls were drawn up and so ready to explode from my need.

I was ready to fill her up, to make her take it all. Then I'd slowly pull out of her and watch as my cum slipped from her pussy.

I groaned out loud from that thought and image.

"Do you fucking want this in you, baby?" I said more crudely. "You want me to pop that cherry of yours, to stretch you all nice and good?"

"Oh. God," she moaned. She nodded.

Yeah, she was ready for me, and I wasn't going to torment either of us any longer.

I was in front of her a second later, gripping her ass cheeks in my hands and lifting her off the ground. She wrapped her legs around my waist, and, holding her ass with one hand, I used the other to grip her long dark hair around my fingers. I yanked her head back, exposing her throat, and while I latched my mouth onto the slender column of her neck, I turned and made my way toward the bed.

I didn't want to let her go, but I also wanted between her sweet thighs even more.

When she was on the center of the bed, her legs slightly parted and her pussy right there for me to see, I knew I wouldn't be able to last very long this first time. It had been years since I was with a woman, and even then no one compared to what I felt for Lexi. My arousal for her had been slowly building from the moment I saw her. Once I was balls-deep in her cunt, I wouldn't last.

But I have all damn day and night to make up for that.

Control. I need to keep my fucking control, or I'll lose it and really scare the fuck out of her.

"I'm about to destroy you, Lexi," I said, meaning it in the best possible way. At least I hoped she understood what I meant. As it was I was walking on a razor wire in holding myself in check.

I got out of my clothes, watching her the whole time, making sure she stayed right there for me, right in the damn zone of being primed.

When I was naked, I grabbed my dick and stroked myself. It felt incredible, especially knowing what I'd be doing very soon, and knowing Lexi was right in front of me in the flesh.

"Spread wider for me. Let me see that untouched pussy, baby." Yeah, I was being a dirty bastard, but I couldn't help it. This was who I was, and I could see she liked it. She did as I asked right away, and I clenched my jaw at how wet she was.

She was glistening for me.

I started stroking myself from root to tip and using the pre-cum that formed at the crown to lubricate my length. My bicep clenched for how strung tight my muscles were. I kept my focus on her pussy, her pink, slightly swollen pussy lips, and the little clit at the top. Sweat was already starting to bead at my brow. Hell, I'd be lucky to last five minutes once inside of her.

I ran my palm over the crest of my cock again, my whole body tense, my breathing ragged.

"Touch yourself," I gritted out between clenched teeth. "I want to see your finger circling that little opening, showing me where I'll be buried soon enough." She listened to me instantly, and all I could do was watch in rapt awe as she touched herself. It was the hottest thing I'd ever seen.

Her hand shook, her belly concaving with every in-hale she made, and I knew she was on the edge, too. If I made her touch her clit, rub that little bud furiously, would she come for me?

I need to find out.

"Touch yourself. I want to see you become un-hinged." She hesitated, and I wondered if she'd touched her pussy before. I took a step closer. "Have you played with yourself, Lexi?" I continued to stroke my shaft. "Have you played with your pussy? Made yourself feel good? Come thinking of dirty thoughts?"

She didn't answer right away, but then she finally nodded. "Tell me about it," I said gruffly, my voice thick. "But move your hand between your legs, rub your clit while you do it."

She took in a stuttering breath.

"Do it. Let me watch you." I was just a foot from her now, the scent of her sweet musk filling my head.

I knew she wouldn't deny me, because no matter how nervous she was, she wanted this, too.

Lexi

"Don't make me repeat myself," Dillon said in this low, husky, but demanding voice.

He wanted me to tell him how I played with myself, while doing that ... getting off for him. I was nervous but so aroused I didn't feel shy or embarrassed about being so wanton. I parted my legs even wider, if that was possible, and did what he wanted. I showed Dillon the most intimate part of me, the area between my thighs that was wet and aching for him.

I wanted to please him.

I looked down at the long, thick length of his cock. He was so big, so hard for me.

I slipped my hand down my belly and stopped when I got to my clit. He kept his focus on me while he jerked off, and that made this harder.

I felt my cheeks heat as I thought about saying how I touched myself ... while he watched and touched himself.

"Say it," he whispered.

God, how did we go from me hitting my head to being in his bed naked?

Why am I even wondering that? This is exactly where I want to be.

"I lay in my bed, smooth my hand over my stomach, and touch myself right here." I rubbed my clit, and a gasp of pleasure left me.

"What do you think about when you do that?" He was moving his palm faster over himself.

My heart beat so hard it ached. I kept touching myself, my pussy so slick my fingers glided over my clit. "You."

His focus was on my splayed thighs, and I saw the pre-cum that dotted the crown of his cock. "Say it again," he ground out.

I moved my finger to my clit and started rubbing the bud harder, faster. I clenched my other hand on the sheets beside me, my back arched, my lips parted. A gasp left me as the pleasure slammed into me. Here we were, watching each other touch ourselves, the eroticism so tangible I felt it lick over my skin.

"I think of you when I touch myself."

He groaned. "Damn, I can't wait."

Before I knew what he was doing, he was running his thumb over the tip of his cock. He was in front of me a second later, eating up the small distance that had separated us.

He reached out, and at the first touch of that digit to my mouth, I gasped.

"Lick it off," he demanded, his voice hard like steel, sharp like a blade.

I ran my tongue along the pad of his thumb, lapping at the saltiness of the cum that was on it. He tasted good, so potent and manly that a fresh wave of desire slammed into me. I got even wetter, which seemed impossible, but the feeling of a fresh gush of moisture didn't lie about my need for him.

He shoved his thumb farther into my mouth, making me lick every last drop of cum from the digit. He stared right into my eyes the whole time, and that made the whole situation even more erotic.

"You like the taste of me on your tongue?"

I nodded, not able to speak with his finger still in my mouth.

"One day I'll have my cock in there, Lexi, and I'll make you swallow my load."

My pulse jacked higher.

"But right now I need to fuck you." He removed his thumb, and I watched in rapt attention as he sucked on it, taking my flavor into his mouth. "I hope you're ready, because there isn't any going back."

He was still stroking himself, and I watched as his bicep contracted and relaxed from the rapid motion.

"Be with me," I said softly, hoping that would end this sexual torment and have Dillon already. As much as I enjoyed the foreplay, I desperately wanted to feel him.

He groaned, took his hand off his dick, and finally moved onto the bed. He used his massive chest to push me back on the mattress, and it felt so good having his weight beside me. For long seconds we didn't say anything, but the sexual chemistry was off the charts intense. I wanted to touch him, to run my hands over his hard body, but a case of nerves suddenly slammed into me. I had never done this before, and no amount of fantasizing about it could give me the courage to just do it.

"I'm going to be your first." He cupped the side of my face, not gently and not like we were about to make love. He touched me like he owned me, like he'd possess every single inch of my body and then some.

And he will. God, he so will.

"I'm going to take your virginity as my own." He slipped his hand down my neck, over my chest, along my belly, and placed it right between my legs over my pussy. "And no other man will know how wet and hot you are here." He added a bit of pressure, and my back arched on its own. "My cock will be the only one that knows exactly how tight your cunt is." He ran his finger up my slit, gathering my wetness and making me moan for him. "I'm going to fill you with my cum, make you so full of it the sheet will be soaked beneath you." He leaned in, his lips right by mine. "But you'll like it. You'll beg me to fill you up every night." His lips brushed against mine. "And I will, because I won't be able to help myself." His voice was low, dark. He started slowly grinding his dick against the side of my thigh. His hand was back at my head, his fingers tangled in my hair. "Say you're mine," he growled out, the wild streak in him fully at the surface.

"I'm yours," I said without hesitation.

"I want you so fucking badly." He tilted my head to the side and started sucking at the base of my throat. God, I could probably have an orgasm from that alone. "After tonight there's no going back."

Good.

He looked into my face again. He leaned in close but didn't kiss me like I desperately wanted him to. "Fuck, you're so fucking gorgeous."

Heat spread through me at his compliment.

I wish I hadn't waited years to come to terms with what I wanted in my life.

"Me either, baby. Me either."

I hadn't realized I'd said my thoughts out loud until he spoke the same thing.

I was done being afraid of my desires, of being nervous of the unknown. I was here with Dillon, and I was going to go after what my heart and body wanted ... him. "Kiss me."

Dillon didn't make either of us wait. He had his mouth on mine seconds later. I couldn't stop the small noise that left the back of my throat.

He made this distorted sound, this all-male, animalistic noise that told me he'd gone over the edge.

This might be my first time, but I wanted him the way I knew he was: raw, rough, uninhibited.

With his hand still in my hair and my throat arched, he broke the kiss and started kissing and sucking the side of my neck again. He was thorough with his tongue and lips, and I was ready to beg him to fuck me.

"You feel what you do to me?" he asked and thrust his dick against my leg harder, firmer.

I nodded, feeling lost.

"You want me to make you feel good?"

"God, yes," I moaned out.

He was on me in the next second.

The hot, hard length of him pressed between my thighs, and I shifted, spreading my legs even wider. His cock pressed right to my slit, and I gasped at how big he was.

Dillon started moving his hips back and forth, rubbing himself against my clit.

I could get off from this alone.

His cockhead moved over my clit every time he pressed his dick upward, and these inaudible sounds left me. I wasn't in control right now. But then again I didn't want to be.

For long seconds all Dillon did was move back and forth against me, driving my lust higher. I had my hands on his biceps, dug my nails into his flesh, and heard him hiss. But as I was about to remove my fingers from his flesh, he grunted.

"No, I like it. Keep them there. Dig your nails in." He thrust against me hard, pressing on my clit.

"How much do you want me right here?" He thrust again, and again, and God, once more. "How much do you want my big dick deep in your pussy?" he whispered by my ear. "You want me stretching this little pussy?"

I nodded, my eyes now closed, my breathing increased.

"You want it to hurt so fucking good?"

I moaned when he pressed his weight down on me farther.

"I want that and more."

He groaned deeply, the noise more pained than anything I'd ever heard before.

"Then hang on, baby, because I'm about to give you more than you can handle."

He reached between our bodies, grabbed his cock, and placed the tip at the entrance of my pussy. Yes, this was what I'd been dying to feel.

Everything inside of me stilled, became tense and ready.

"Relax for me," he said softly by my ear.

I did as he said, but I knew if I just shifted a little, I could impale myself on him.

"There is no going back."

"I don't want to go back, Dillon." And I didn't. "I don't want slow and romantic. I want fast and hard. I want it the way you want to give it to me."

"Because that's the way you want it, too. Yeah?"

I nodded. "Yeah."

He didn't move for a second, but I felt how wide the head of his dick was pressed against me. This would be painful at first, but I was so wet, so worked up, I knew I wouldn't stop this, knew I'd explode for him like a rocket.

There really was no going back.

In one deep, hard thrust, he shoved all those huge inches into me. My back arched involuntary from the sudden motion, from the powerful penetration. My breasts were thrust out, my nipples rock hard. The pain was there, sharp, claiming my entire body. I was stretched in two by him. Dillon was just so large, so thick, there was no going around the discomfort.

He groaned above me, closed his eyes, beads of sweat on his forehead. He was tense, his muscles strained, his tendons on display.

He's trying to control himself.

His balls were pressed right up against my ass. They were a big, heavy weight.

But then he started pulling out and gently pushing back in. The pain mixed with the pleasure, and I felt ecstasy move through me and settle in my cells.

As the seconds moved on, the minutes being eaten up, his motions became fiercer, more determined.

He had his eyes partially open, his focus on me. His massive chest rose and fell as he breathed in and out, brushing against mine, letting reality settle in further.

"Fuck, yeah, baby." He pushed in deep, so deep I was rocked up on the bed an inch. He pulled out, bringing the tip of himself right to my entrance. He plunged back in, taking my sanity, the very self-awareness from me.

"Watch as I take you, as I claim this pussy as my own." He slammed into me again but then rose up, his forearms going straight, his head downcast as he looked at where we were connected. "Hell, baby," he said, low, husky.

I shifted slightly, seeing what he did. I watched as he pumped in and out of me, his cock becoming visible. His length was covered in my juices, and I saw streaks of my virgin blood covering him.

Why that sight turned me on even more was lost on me, but God, it was hot.

When I lifted my head and looked at his face again, I saw Dillon was already watching me.

"Knowing you're watching what I'm doing, how I'm fucking you..." His body shook atop mine as if he was having a hard time controlling the action. "Turns me on like a motherfucker."

I lay back down and just let him do this ... do me.

It was as if that one action was what he needed to go primal on me. Dillon started fucking me like he really meant it, and I hadn't realized until this one moment just how much he'd been holding back.

He pulled out of me, and I gasped in surprise and at the loss of having him buried in my body. But before I could complain or beg him to slide back into my pussy, he gripped my waist and flipped me over.

"So damn perfect." He didn't make me wait long to feel those monstrous inches again. I closed my eyes and curled the sheets in my fists, loving the sensation his palms on my ass conjured in me.

Feels good.

"I hope you're ready," he said in this hard, dangerous voice. "Get on your hands and knees, present yourself to me." I did as he said, my pussy already feeling sore though he hadn't even been inside me that long. But damn, I wanted to feel that discomfort, wanted to remember exactly how deep he had been in me.

When I was in position, he forcefully pushed my legs farther apart. Did he know how much I liked that? Did he know him being rough made this even better for me?

He smoothed his hand over my ass. His touch felt so good, so demanding. There was no doubt in my mind that Dillon was all raw sex and hardcore desires. For long seconds all he did was stroke my ass, but then he brought his palm down on it hard, and I gasped out. He did it again, groaned deeply in his chest, and I jerked and gasped in pleasure.

"Lexi. Mine."

I'd never get sick of hearing him say my name or declaring what he wanted ... me.

"You're so fucking hot." He grabbed a chunk of my hair forcefully, and I moaned in response. Dillon yanked my head back, getting more leverage, and growled low. "You want me back inside?"

"Yes." I all but cried out that lone word.

He placed his cock right back at my entrance and in a fluid motion shoved deep into me.

"*Jesus.*"

Dillon started picking up speed and soon was fucking me with abandon.

"Yes," I found myself crying out.

He grabbed my waist, curled his fingers into my flesh hard enough it hurt, and fucked me like he was dying for it.

"Fuck. Yeah. Lexi."

Over and over he surged into me and retreated. And when I couldn't take any more, when I felt the world fall away, he plunged into me once more and stilled.

"So damn good," he gritted out. "I'm coming."

I came right along with him.

He filled me up with so much of his cum I knew I'd feel it slip out of me when I stood. I'd be forever marked by him.

He jerked above me, still coming, still groaning. "Shit, baby." The words sounded distorted, out of breath.

It seemed like our combined pleasure went on for ages, but just when I caught my breath, he sagged, his cock still hard in me, his flesh damp on mine. He pulled out, and we both made this disgruntled sound. I couldn't stop myself from collapsing onto the mattress, the sheets smelling like him and making me feel drunk. The bed shifted as he lay down beside me. The sensation of his hand on my back, of his big strong fingers caressing me, had calm settling over me.

I felt myself start to come down from the high, but as soon as Dillon placed his hand between my legs and rested it right over my pussy, my body heated again.

"Mine, Lexi."

Yeah, I am.

"God, baby."

Dillon was breathing just as hard as I was. He pulled me close to the warmth of his body and grabbed the blanket to cover us. This didn't feel like some awkward after-sex thing. It felt right, comfortable, like I was exactly where I should be.

"I'm not letting you go."

Heat filled me, and it had nothing to do with being aroused still. I shifted so I could look at his face and see how serious he was. His dark eyes were so expressive in this moment.

"You're probably thinking this is pretty fucking fast and crazy."

I was, but I wanted it that way.

"But when I say I'm not letting you go, I mean it. Do you understand what that means?"

"I hope I know what it means," I said truthfully.

"It means you're mine. It means I want you here, by my side." He cupped my cheek and stared into my eyes. "It means that no matter what, you're it for me. I'm tired of being alone, and you're the one I want."

I might not know what the future held, but what I did know with certainty was that this man was who I wanted to be with. We completed each other in a way that no one else could match. He filled that lonely hole I'd had for so long, and I felt I did the same for him.

We didn't have to be strangers moving through life with just the purpose of being alive.

We could actually *live*.

I didn't want to let that go.
I wouldn't let him go.

CHAPTER EIGHT

Lexi

The next day

"I want to stay like this, Lexi, with you in my bed, under my roof," Dillon said, his voice deep and sleep filled. "I want you to be mine in every conceivable way, not because I'd keep you here—which has crossed my mind—but because you know this is where you're supposed to be." His words were genuine, serious. He had his hand right between my legs, his palm covering my pussy. It was this act of ownership, and it made me feel good.

I didn't feel like a piece of property to Dillon, not with the way he held me, and not with the words he spoke. This was fast, maybe even insane, but it felt right.

I'd come here looking for answers, looking for something that would bring realization and reality into my life. I'd hoped I'd find that with Dillon, and that my instincts hadn't been wrong in thinking we were two of the same.

I shifted on the bed so I could face him. He had this intense look on his face, but I'd come to realize that was just Dillon. He was hard in all ways, closed off from his emotions after whatever he'd gone through. I felt the product of his desire for me, his cock still so hard, so big. We might have just had sex, but it seemed like he was still ready for me, still needing me.

But when I shifted closer, he placed a hand on my neck, not adding pressure but stopping me, being proprietary.

"Do you want this?" he asked softly.

"I want this," I said without question. Maybe this was too soon, too deep? But we'd just had sex. Surely being that intimate with a man, hearing the way he spoke about me and the things he wanted with me, meant this wasn't just about being together physically?

He cupped my cheek and for long seconds said nothing. The feel of his thumb moving along my skin, soft, gentle, told me this man, despite his fierceness, was a gentle giant.

But only to you.

I knew that. I felt it.

I looked at his inner bicep and saw a small black sparrow tattoo. Not thinking, just acting, I lifted my hand and touched that small design.

"What does it mean?"

He was silent for a second. "The freedom I know my brother would want for me, but that I can't give in to."

I stared into his face, saw his expression clouded with whatever he was currently thinking about.

Even I could see the symbolism of the darkness of the little bird, of the lack of dimension, life.

"You can have whatever you want."

His face softened just a fraction, and he leaned in and kissed me. "I have you. That's all I need."

I melted against him, and for long seconds I just rested my head on his chest and listened to the sound of his heart beating.

"Can you live with that in a man?"

I didn't need to elaborate on what he meant. I knew. I tipped my head back and stared into his face once more. "I came here because I saw something in you I saw in myself each and every day." I placed my hand on his stubble-covered cheek. "I'm not looking to change you. Who you are is what I want. You're who I want." I went back to resting my head on his chest, and we stayed like that, not speaking, just breathing.

Just living.

Dillon

I listened to the sound of Lexi sleeping. I watched the rise and fall of her chest as she breathed. Her face was unmarred by the fact she rested, was content and peaceful. She knew she was safe with me. I could sense it, feel it in the way she relaxed against me.

I smoothed my hand down her side, along the dip of her waist, over her hip, and along her ass.

She was mine in all ways.

I wouldn't let her go.

She'd accept who I was, that I wasn't the "good guy." I'd go to hell to protect her, and take anyone with me that thought to hurt her, but I'd never be that knight in shining armor that rode in on a white horse to save the day.

I was more aptly the monster in a horror movie.

I could never submit to my darkness. It just dissolved into background noise because she was in my life.

It was true that with her I felt this calm, this easiness I'd never felt before. But I'd seen too much, in life and in war; I'd never be able to be the man she deserved.

But I'd strive each and every day to make her see, to let her know she was the only thing that mattered to me. Without her in my life I was just walking around with that cloud of hatred and self-loathing hanging over my head.

With her by my side I felt a semblance of being complete. This was fast, maybe even a little on the crazy side, but I lived for that … I'd live for her.

I might not be able to change who I was, but I could make damn sure I gave her a happy life and that she knew she came first. Always.

CHAPTER NINE

Dillon

One week later

I wanted to keep her here, forgetting about the ugly world just beyond this cabin in the woods. But Lexi needed to come to that realization on her own. She needed to see that what we could have here was all we needed.

I wanted Lexi to know that if she stayed with me, that would be it. There was no going back, no hoping I could change, live the life she'd once led.

I'd never change.

I'd always be possessive of her.

I'd always keep her close.

I drove us down the mountain, the road rocky, uneven. I sensed she was nervous, and reached across the seat to pull her closer. Hell, if I could have had her on my lap, I would have gone that route.

I wanted to ask her if she was sure, if this was what she wanted. But I knew the answer already. I knew she was right here with me.

And fuck, did it feel good.

It was another half hour before we finally reached her place. I stayed in the driver's seat, letting her lead. This was her call, and she held the power. If she decided she didn't want the only life I could give her, I could pretend I'd let that be the final say. But the truth was I couldn't let her go, ever.

I stayed silent and stared at her, seeing the thoughts moving across her face in an expressive kaleidoscope.

And for the first time in my life, when I knew she could change her mind right here, right now, I felt fear.

Lexi

It smelled the same, a mixture of regret, sadness, but of memories, too.

I'd gotten the courage to get out of the car and go through with this. I stared at the home I'd grown up in, the house where I'd had laughs, scares, and cries. This used to be a home, but now it just felt like a shell: empty, lonely.

I felt Dillon place his hand on my shoulder, and the warmth of it, the stability ... the fact that I wasn't alone, had already told me ten times over that my decision had been the right call.

There was no way I'd ignore how I felt or what I wanted in my life. I firmly believed I'd been put in Dillon's path—and vice versa—for a reason.

This was where I lived, where I once had my home, but not anymore.

I turned and rose on my toes, placing my lips on Dillon's. He wrapped his arms around me, holding me close, making me feel all kinds of comfort and love.

Yes. Love.

I craned my head back and stared into Dillon's face. He looked conflicted, and I'd even go as far as saying worried.

"This isn't where my life is anymore." In that second I saw the change in his expression instantly.

Relief.

"I want my home to be with you, because that's where I'm meant to be."

Fast was an understatement on how things had gone with Dillon, but it felt like a missing puzzle piece in my life had been found. He lifted his hand and gently touched the cut on my head from when I fell. I was fine, but I could see on his face it was something small like that that could unravel his hard composure.

"I want you to be sure." His voice sounded even more hard than normal, pained even.

"I'm sure." And I was.

"Good, because no way could I walk away from you." He kissed my forehead. "No fucking way I could lose you when I just now have you." He cupped my cheeks and looked into my eyes. "I don't know if I can give you that fairy-tale life, but I sure as hell know I can make you happy."

That made me feel all kinds of pleasurable things. "You already are."

I'd figure out what to do about my once-life in town. I didn't want to be here, hadn't even before I decided to just follow my heart and go to Dillon. This place had lost its appeal a long time ago.

I'd figure things out soon enough, but right now my happiness—and Dillon's—was what mattered.

What was the point of life if you couldn't be happy with the one you wanted?

EPILOGUE ONE

Dillon

One year later

I stared at Lexi through the window. She couldn't see me, not with the light inside and the darkness out. But I saw her perfectly. I saw everything that made up my life when I looked at her, that made me feel whole once again. It was her that brought me back from that ledge. Although I'd always be dark, always keep to myself, she was the only one that I would ever open up to.

We were one and the same, she and I.

She is mine.

My woman.

The woman I love more than life itself.

My wife.

She'd always been mine, and she always would be.

We'd gotten married months ago. It hadn't been anything fancy. Hell, we didn't actually have family or friends that could have attended if it was anyway. No, we did the whole courthouse thing, and our honeymoon was staying in bed, naked, exhausted from fucking, for an entire week.

God, that had been incredible. We'd fed each other, been sweaty from making love numerous times a day, and when we weren't being together, we just talked.

We talked about anything and everything.

A sigh of contented happiness left me.

I liked having her to myself, and us being out here alone.

If anyone were stupid enough to try and take that from me, to try and get between us, they'd find out exactly how possessive I was about her. If they tried to hurt the one person I cared about more than fucking life itself … they'd find out I wasn't afraid to break bones and shed blood.

I didn't care if it was extreme.

I didn't care if it was obsession that drove me.

I fucking loved her, and that would never change.

I grabbed a few logs for the fire and made my way back into the cabin. It was starting to snow again, and the weather was frigid. It was already a cold fucking winter, and it would only get worse over the next few months.

I got inside, went over to the fire to add more wood and stoke it, then turned and stared at Lexi.

Mine.

She was still looking out the window, the wind now picking up and casting ice and snow against the glass. I lowered my gaze to her belly. She was five months along now, my baby growing inside of her.

Pride and possessiveness slammed into me, with a good dose of protectiveness.

My woman.

My child.

I went over to her and pulled her into my arms. For long seconds I just held her and rubbed my hand over her back. "What are you thinking about?" I asked. I inhaled deeply, smelling the sweet scent of the shampoo she used. My cock punched forward, but then again, it didn't take much for the fucker to get hard where Lexi was concerned. All I had to do was think about her and I was ready to breed her.

"Just thinking about how far we've come this past year."

We had come far. "But you're happy?"

"Of course."

"And you don't regret any of it?"

She shook her head, and the softest, sweetest smile covered her face.

I leaned down to kiss her. "Did you ever see yourself here?" I placed my hand between us on her belly. She nodded.

"I wanted to, Dillon."

I kissed her harder. "What did you see, baby?" I cupped the back of her head and brought it to my chest. She rested it there for long seconds before speaking.

"I saw myself not being alone." She pulled back and looked at me. "I saw myself with someone who was just like me."

God, this woman could bring me to my fucking knees.

"I saw someone who was an outcast, who had no one on his side, and I wanted to be the person that gave you something more. I wanted to be the person that had more."

I did fall to my knees then, pushing her shirt up and exposing her growing belly. I kissed her stomach over and over again before resting my forehead on it. I closed my eyes, not sure what a fucker like me had done to deserve a woman like Lexi.

"You're the one that made me the person I am today." I didn't care how sappy any of this shit was. This was the truth, and I'd say it until I had no air in my lungs. "You're the only one who could break through me and ease that feral quality I held tightly to me like armor."

She ran her hands through my hair and shook her head. "You and I both know I didn't tame any of your wildness." She smiled and kept running her fingers through the strands on my head.

But she had tamed me … partly. I might be one possessive and territorial bastard where it concerned her and the child she carried, but before her I hadn't given a shit about anyone or anything. Not even myself.

"Before you I was just surviving." I placed a hand on either side of her belly and kissed her skin. She was warm and so soft. "You made me want to live," I whispered against her stomach. "I want to be a good man for you, and a good father for our baby." Before Lexi I'd just been a shell.

"You'll be the best father, Dillon, and you're already a good man for me. You're the best."

I rose up and hugged her, keeping her close, making sure she knew she was safe.

Because of Lexi I became a man.

I became a real man with a purpose.

Lexi

I wanted to smile at the protectiveness that came from Dillon.

He carried the car seat that held our son, Rowley. He had this scowl on his face as we made our way through the grocery store.

It had only been three months since I had our son, and this was the first trip down the mountain and into town. It was monthly supply stocking time, and although Dillon would have been happy to keep the baby and me at home, I wanted to come.

This had been my home, after all.

"I can put the car seat in the cart, you know?" I chuckled when I saw his knuckles turn white on the handle as he held the baby carrier tighter.

An older woman with her husband purposefully moved to the side for us, and Dillon grunted.

This might have been my home at one time, but not anymore. My home was where Rowley and Dillon were. I'd left this all behind, made a life for myself away from it all.

And when our children were old enough for school, were old enough to decide what they wanted, then we'd take that step. We'd do what was best for us and not what others thought.

We went to check out, and I felt eyes on us from all directions. And I lifted my head and looked at each and every one of them. I could have said something, anything to them, but they didn't matter. Nothing mattered aside from Dillon and our son.

Mary was working the register, and I wish I could have taken a picture of her face in this moment: wide eyes and a look like she was a fish out of water. I remembered all the shit she'd talked about Dillon when he came in, and I wanted nothing more than to say something smug. But I was better than that.

Dillon wrapped his arm around me and pulled me close, the proprietary mark being made known.

That made me feel so good, so loved. It also made me feel like a woman owned.

Dillon leaned down and whispered in my ear, "Because I do own you, baby."

I felt my face heat. I'd either said that out loud, or he knew me too well. Either way I wasn't embarrassed.

I was pleased.

When we left the store, I felt everyone still watching us.

"I want to go back in there and really give them something to stare at."

We put the baby in the back, and I turned and faced him. "Let them stare. Let them talk. They'll never have what we do." He had me wrapped in his arms a second later.

He kissed me in front of everyone, and all I did was hold on as he took possession of me. "No, they'll never have what we do. No one can ever have what we have, Lexi."

That was the truth.

When I moved back, I saw Dillon had gone tense, his focus on something behind me. I looked over my shoulder and saw a man standing there, a cigarette between his lips, his focus on me.

There hadn't been many times where Dillon's possessiveness came through concerning an actual person since we lived away from people, but right now I knew this was what truly living was about.

He was jealous and wanted to stake his claim.

I felt Dillon move his hand down the length of my spine, over the small of my back, and finally along the curve of my ass. Truth was I liked this caveman attitude he had going on. I loved that he wanted it known I was his. The look on Dillon's face was pretty dangerous, and if I'd been that guy my man's focus was on, I would have hauled ass inside.

Dillon's attitude right now screamed "*mine*" in every single way.

The guy finally looked away after a second and made his way inside the store.

All I could do was smile and let those butterflies in my belly continue to warm me.

My man loved me to the ends of the earth.

He gave my ass a smack, and I chuckled. Of course he had to get that last thing in.

We got in the vehicle and headed back to our home. I couldn't help but stare at the man that had opened my eyes to so much, to a world that was unlike anything I'd ever imagined. What we had might not have been conventional to some, and people might talk. But when you have the love of a man, and the knowledge that he'd move heaven and hell to make sure you're happy, there was nothing that could ruin that.

He pulled me closer, and I rested my head on his shoulder. The baby made little grunting noises, and I smiled.

"I love you," I said softly.

Dillon made a low sound. "And I fucking love you, baby."

Yeah, perfection was what we made of it.

It was the love of a man, and the feeling of your child in your arms. I knew that just because things were dark, that didn't mean it was bad. It just meant the light hadn't reached it yet.

EPILOGUE TWO

Dillon

Considering where I started, what I'd lost, and where I'd been, my life was pretty fucking incredible. I had the one woman who "got me," who knew where I was coming from and accepted me no matter what. I had a healthy baby boy, and hopefully more on the way.

I had love despite still having darkness in me.

I bought my hammer down on the nail, securing the slab of wood to the frame. I did this over and over again, the sound of contact from the tool echoing off the trees. When the sun started to set, I put my tools away and took a step back to eye the work that was done so far. We were expanding on the cabin, making it bigger, hoping to fill it with a family. It would take a long fucking time for sure, but that's all we had, and I looked forward to it.

Maybe just moving into town would have been easier, buying a two-story with a white picket, four bedrooms, and a family room. But that's not who I was, and I knew that wasn't how my wife was either. This was the type of living we wanted and needed.

I glanced at the living room window. I thought about a year ago when I'd been standing almost in this exact place, and looked to see Lexi standing on the other side of the glass.

And look where we are now.

My emotions for her were genuine. Authentic.

My love for her was fierce, untamed.

And my desire for her was feral and uninhibited.

True, I was sweaty and exhausted from working all day on the cabin extension, but just looking at her had me rock hard.

I need her.

I went inside and immediately glanced over at the basinet. The baby was sound asleep, a fire was cracking and roaring in the hearth, and my woman was looking at me like she knew exactly what I wanted.

She's looking at me like she wants the same thing I do.

We didn't say anything, just started getting undressed. I was covered in sweat, smelling like lumber, but hell, I knew my girl liked that.

When I was naked and she was just in her bra and panties, I grabbed my cock and stroked myself. "Take it all off for me," I said softly.

She pushed her underwear down, then went for her bra. And when Lexi was stark naked, I moved closer. No way in fuck was I going to do foreplay tonight. This was going to be rough, hard, and nothing would be held back.

I crooked my finger at her and made her come to me, made her eat up that foot between us. I had her in my arms a second later and moved over to the kitchen table. I kissed her for a long second, running my tongue along her lips, plunging it into her mouth. When I broke away, it was to turn her around, press my hand on the center of her back, and shove her forward. I kicked her legs out and leaned back to look at her exposed pussy.

"Fuck, baby," I groaned.

When I ran my fingers through her wet slit and heard her moan softly, I knew there was no way I was going to last once I was in her.

I'd come within five minutes.

"Tell me what you want."

"You."

"You want my big cock in your tight little pussy, baby?"

She nodded. "God, yes." She was breathless when she said that.

"This is going to be fast and hard, and I won't last."

"Good, because I'm already right there, Dillon."

I groaned low.

I gripped her ass and spread it wide, taking a long look at the pink, soaking center of her cunt.

My cock jerked again, and my balls drew up tight. I needed this like I needed to breathe.

Taking my cock in hand, I led the head to her pussy hole.

"Yes," she whispered. "Fuck me."

I grabbed her hair, yanked her head back, baring her throat, and plunged my cock into her in one hard, thorough thrust. She arched her back and opened her mouth on a silent cry. I felt her cunt stretch around me. She made a deep noise in the back of her throat.

"Fuck yes." And then I became a fucking beast with her.

I pulled out, and when the tip was at the entrance, I shoved back in hard. Her upper body slid on the table from the force. Her pussy was so tight, so wet and hot.

The sound of my flesh slapping hers filled my head.

"Damn, I'm not going to last," I grunted. I grabbed her hips, digging my fingers into her flesh.

"I'm so close." She all but moaned those words out.

Christ.

I reached around and found her clit with my finger. I teased that little bundle, knowing she'd get off for me. I plunged my cock in and out of her at the same time I rubbed her clit back and forth. I needed her to come for me more than once. I needed to feel her pussy clamping down on my shaft. She cried my name softly right before she finally got off for me.

That's all I needed to follow suit.

I buried my dick in her and came so damn hard I saw stars.

"Take all of me, Lexi baby."

"Yes," she cried out softly, mindful of the baby sleeping.

I leaned forward, took hold of her chin with my thumb and forefinger, and turned her head more to the side. Her lips were parted, and her eyes were heavy-lidded. I leaned down and slammed my mouth onto hers, claiming it as mine, plunging my tongue in the warm, wet depth, and fucking her there like I was between her thighs.

My orgasm was fierce and strong, and I filled her up with my cum.

The pleasure started to soften as my peak lowered. Long moments passed where neither of us moved. Then again I liked being buried in her, my cock softening, her warmth surrounding me.

I forced myself to pull out of her, not because I wanted to but because the position had to be uncomfortable for her. I had her turned around and in my arms just a second later. She rested her head on my shoulder.

"I love you," I said against the side of her head and inhaled the sweet scent of her hair. "You love me too?" I teased.

"So much it hurts."

Yeah, she was exactly where she was meant to be.

With me.

Always.

The End

OUT NOW

Say You're Mine

Say You're Mine

USA TODAY BESTSELLING AUTHOR
JENIKA SNOW

CHAPTER ONE

Felix

Six years old

The first time I saw you I knew you were mine.

When she walked into the room, everything around me disappeared. It felt as if was just the two of us.

She was the prettiest girl I'd ever seen, even though her clothes seemed a little too baggy, had stains on them, and holes, too"

Yeah, she was the prettiest girl in the whole world.

I didn't even know her name because the teacher hadn't introduced her to the class yet, but I didn't care.

I knew I wanted to be her friend.

I knew I wanted her to always be near me.

"Class, this is Maggie. She's come all the way to Ohio from Colorado." The teacher touched Maggie's shoulder and smiled at us. "I want you all to make Maggie feel welcome."

I followed Maggie with my gaze as she went to the other side of the room, and finally sat down behind an empty desk. The other kids ignored her, busy working on their paintings.

Her hair was the color of the sun, in two pigtails. I couldn't stop staring at her. I didn't want to. She glanced up at me then, her eyes so big, so blue, they reminded me of the ocean we had just learned about. I hated that she looked sad, that no one was sitting beside her, talking to her.

I had to fix that.

Grabbing my paper and watercolors, I walked over to where she sat. The other kids looked up at me, but I was only focusing on Maggie.

When I sat beside her, I saw her eyes widen even farther.

"Hi," I said, smiling, hoping she wouldn't be scared to be here anymore. "I'm Felix."

She didn't say anything right away and instead looked down at the art supplies I'd brought with me.

I couldn't understand what I felt, but I knew I wanted her to be my friend. I wanted us to be best friends.

"Maggie," she said softly. She looked up then, her blue eyes pretty but still scared.

"Wanna be friends?" I smiled. I hoped she wouldn't laugh at the missing front tooth I had. I'd just lost it and put it under my pillow for the tooth fairy. I'd gotten a whole dollar for it.

She shrugged and looked down at the table again.

"You can think about it, but I'm really nice, and I won't let anyone be mean to you." She looked up again and smiled. It wasn't a big one, but it was a smile just for me. "Hey, you're missing a tooth, too." I pointed to my missing tooth. She stopped smiling, and I felt bad for saying something. "See?" I smiled wider, pointing out the big gap between my teeth. "I lost mine a couple days ago. I got a lot from the tooth fairy." She didn't say anything. "How much did you get?"

She shook her head. "The tooth fairy doesn't come to my house."

"Why not?"

She didn't say anything for a long time. "The tooth fairy doesn't like coming to my house because it's dirty and my mom and dad fight a lot. She's never come to my house, not even when my big brother lost teeth."

I didn't like that at all.

She glanced at me again, and the way she seemed so scared had something inside of me hurting.

I tried to think of what I could do to make her feel better, and then I looked down at the paper and watercolors in front of me.

I grabbed my brush, dipped it in the cup of water the teacher had put on the table, and picked the color I wanted. I knew she watched me. I could feel her eyes on me, and I liked that.

When I was finished, I stared at my picture before handing it to her. Maggie reached out and took it, and for long seconds just stared at it.

"This is for me?" she asked.

I nodded, feeling proud of myself. What I did know was I was keeping Maggie as mine.

Maggie

He'd drawn a pink heart on the paper. Although it was a little crooked, it was perfect.

He'd made it. Just for me.

I'd never had anyone do anything nice like this for me.

What he wouldn't know was how much a heart on the paper meant to me.

"You and I will be the best of friends," Felix said.

I wanted to be his friend, but I didn't fit in here. My clothes were old, used, and I didn't have nice things like the other girls in the class. Even Felix looked nice, with clothes that didn't have stains on them, or shoes with holes in the side.

"Why would you want to be my friend?" I asked.

He looked at me funny then. "Why wouldn't I want to be your friend?"

I shrugged. "No one ever wants to be my friend." Back at my old school I was called mean things: dirty, poor, ugly. And then Felix reached out and placed his hand over mine. I looked up and stared into his green eyes. They reminded me of grass in the summer.

"I'm gonna be your best friend, Maggie."

I liked how he said my name.

"I'm never letting you go."

And for some reason I really believed him.

OUT NOW: http://amzn.to/2gj2lDV

ABOUT THE AUTHOR

Want to learn more about Jenika Snow? Check her out below...

Web: http://www.jenikasnow.com/

Email: Jenika_Snow@yahoo.com

FB: http://www.facebook.com/jenikasnow

Twitter: http://www.twitter.com/jenikasnow

Crescent Snow Publishing:
http://www.crescentsnowpublishing.com

Instagram: http://instagram.com/jenikasnow

Newsletter: http://eepurl.com/ce7yS-/

39194107R00064

Made in the USA
Middletown, DE
07 January 2017